Disney's THE HUNCHBACK OF NOTRE DAME

Quasimodo's New Friend

By Justine Korman
Illustrated by Serge Michaels
and Edward Gutierrez

 **A GOLDEN BOOK • NEW YORK**

Western Publishing Company, Inc., Racine, Wisconsin 53404

uasimodo lived in the bell tower of Notre Dame cathedral. His cruel master, Judge Frollo, had forbidden him to leave the tower, but Quasimodo's gargoyle friends, Hugo, Victor, and Laverne, kept him company.

One morning, in the busy square below, the friends saw a ball of orange fur streak by, chased by a pack of barking dogs. It was a kitten!

The kitten didn't stop running until it was halfway up Notre Dame. Then it stared down at the square far below and made a tiny "meow."

"Silly kitten! Who told him to go rock climbing?" Hugo said.
"Perhaps it would be wise if . . ." Victor began.
"Oh, the poor thing," said Laverne.

But Quasimodo was already on his way to rescue the
frightened kitten.

Safely inside the bell tower, the kitten purred happily. Quasimodo patted its tiny head. "I will call you Mignon," Quasimodo told him. "It means dainty or sweet. Do you like that?"

As if in answer, the kitten licked Quasimodo's hand.
"He likes me!" Quasimodo cried.
"He's hungry," Hugo said.
"I think . . ." Victor began.

Quasimodo filled a pan with water. The thirsty kitten drank it quickly and yawned. Then he curled himself into a ball and fell fast asleep. Quasimodo had never seen anything so sweet.

As Mignon slept, Quasimodo began to carve a figure of him for his miniature city.

After his nap, Mignon decided to explore the bell tower.
He chased the pigeons and sparrows from one end of the
tower to the other. What fun he was having!

"Watch out!" Quasimodo warned. But it was too late. Mignon crashed into his miniature city. Paint splashed all over Victor. Hugo laughed.

Then the kitten landed on Hugo's house of cards. "That creature has got to go," he said angrily.

Victor dabbed at his face. "I quite agree. In fact . . ."

"The bird chaser stays!" Laverne said.

As Quasimodo straightened up his model city, Mignon
padded silently down the bell tower steps. "Come and see
your figure, Mignon," Quasimodo called to him. But the
kitten was nowhere in sight.

Quasimodo realized that Mignon must have wandered down into the church. He found him just as Frollo entered the sanctuary. Quasimodo quickly hid the kitten under his shirt.

"Quasimodo," said Frollo, "you know you don't belong down here."

Quasimodo squirmed as the kitten wriggled inside his shirt. "Oh . . . yes, Master. I will return right now," he answered, hurrying toward the tower.

Back in the bell tower, Mignon took a little nap, and Quasimodo told his friends what had happened.

"That was a close call," Hugo said.

Victor shook his head. "You can't hide the kitten forever. The best thing would be to get rid . . ."

"No!" Laverne shrieked. "This is the first time I've been bird-free for years!"

"Mignon has a home here as long as he needs one," said Quasimodo, ending the argument.

It was time for Quasimodo to ring the evening bells.
Gong-GONGGGG! the bells chimed.
"Ma-ROOOOW!" Mignon joined in.
The kitten watched the bells swinging back and forth.
He loved the sound of their evening song.

The next morning was cool and quiet. There were no chirping sparrows or cooing pigeons fluttering around the bell tower.

Suddenly, in the silence, Quasimodo heard a little girl's sad voice calling, "Here, kitty, kitty. Here, kitty, kitty."

Mignon's ears perked up when he heard the voice. He raced to the window and gave an answering "MEOW!"

Quasimodo realized that Mignon belonged to the little girl.
Gently he picked him up and climbed down the cathedral. He
placed Mignon next to the girl and hurried back up to the bell
tower.

The girl turned around. "Where have you been?" she exclaimed.

Then, as Mignon and the girl turned to go, the bells of
Notre Dame began to ring.

"Ma-ROOOOW!" Mignon looked back and meowed
loudly in reply.

Up in the bell tower, Quasimodo smiled. He knew that
from now on, whenever he heard the bells of Notre Dame,
Mignon would think of his dear friend Quasimodo.